LOST IN LUMINA

Stella Serene

GLOBAL
PUBLISHING
SOLUTIONS

LOST IN LUMINA by Stella Serene
Published by Global Publishing Solutions, LLC
923 Fieldside Drive
Matteson, Illinois 60443
www.globalpublishingsolutions.com

This book or parts thereof may not be reproduced in any form, stored in a retrieval system, or transmitted in any form by any means—electronic, mechanical, photocopy, recording, or otherwise—without prior permission of the publisher, except as provided by United States of America copyright law.

Copyright © 2024 by Stella Serene

All rights reserved.

International Standard Book Number:
9798330294206
E-book International Standard Book Number:
9798330294213

Unless otherwise indicated, all the names, characters, businesses, places, events, and incidents in this book are either the product of the author's imagination or used in a fictitious manner. Any resemblance to actual persons, living or dead, or actual events is purely coincidental.

Printed in the United States of America

TABLE OF CONTENTS

The Enchanted Forest 1
The Whispering Willows 5
The Journey to the Heart 9
Shadows of the Past 13
The Moonlit Meadow 17
The Forest Keeper 21
The Elemental Realms 24
The Convergence 28
The Shadow's Return 29
The Guardian's Triumph 30
A New Dawn 31

THE ENCHANTED FOREST

Mia, a spirited young woman with insatiable curiosity, found herself on the outskirts of a dense forest that had always been shrouded in mystery. As she stepped beneath the towering canopy, the air seemed to shimmer with an otherworldly energy. Lumina, as the locals whispered, was no ordinary forest.

The first rays of the morning sun filtered through the emerald leaves, casting a dappled glow on the path ahead. Mia's heart quickened with each step, anticipation and wonder fueling her adventurous spirit. Birds chirped in a melodic chorus, welcoming her to the realm of Lumina.

The further she ventured, the more the forest came alive. Glowing orbs floated lazily through the air, emitting a gentle luminescence that bathed the surroundings in an ethereal light. Mia's eyes widened as she encountered creatures with iridescent wings, their delicate forms dancing in harmony with the enchanting melodies that echoed through the woods.

With each passing moment, Lumina revealed itself as a place untouched by the constraints of the mundane. Mia felt a magnetic pull, drawing her deeper into its heart. Strange flowers bloomed in radiant hues she had never seen, releasing fragrances that carried with them the whispers of forgotten tales.

As Mia walked, the very ground beneath her seemed to pulse with an ancient magic. Lumina's energy resonated with her, and an unspoken connection formed between the enchanted realm and the curious adventurer. Mia's senses heightened, attuned to the secrets Lumina held.

The journey unfolded with Mia navigating the meandering paths, encountering creatures that regarded her with curious eyes. The air hummed with anticipation, and Mia couldn't shake the feeling that Lumina held a story waiting to be unveiled. Little did she know that this was only the beginning of an extraordinary journey—one that would intertwine her destiny with the fate of the mystical realm she had stumbled upon.

THE WHISPERING WILLOWS

Mia's journey into Lumina continued, guided by an inexplicable force that seemed to draw her toward the heart of the mystical forest. As she followed a winding path, the towering ancient willow trees loomed in the distance, their long branches swaying in a dance with the unseen breeze.

Approaching the Whispering Willows, Mia felt a sense of reverence. The air was tinged with an ancient wisdom, and the gentle rustle of leaves overhead carried with it the soft murmurings of forgotten tales. Mia hesitated for a moment before stepping into the sacred grove.

Under the willow trees' expansive canopy, Mia felt a hushed energy—a communion of spirits that had witnessed the ebb and flow of Lumina's magic for centuries. As if responding to her presence, the willows began to whisper, their voices weaving together in a chorus of secrets.

The story they revealed was one of a forgotten kingdom, where Lumina once thrived as a beacon of magic and harmony. But, over time, shadows crept in, and the kingdom fell into obscurity. The willows spoke of a prophecy—a tale written in the wind, carried through generations, foretelling the arrival of a seeker who would play a pivotal role in Lumina's destiny.

Mia listened with rapt attention as the willows recounted the challenges faced by Lumina—the loss of its magic, the fading of its brilliance, and the gradual retreat into obscurity. The prophecy hinted at a way to restore Lumina's former glory, and Mia felt a deep connection to the tale, as if the forest itself had chosen her to be the harbinger of change.

In the hallowed grove, surrounded by the whispers of the willows, Mia glimpsed the intricacies of Lumina's past. The weight of responsibility settled on her shoulders, and a determination ignited within her—a resolve to unravel the mysteries of the enchanting realm and to play her part in its restoration.

As Mia stepped out of the Whispering Willows, the forest seemed to echo with the knowledge she had gained. Lumina's secrets beckoned her forward, and with each step, she embraced the unfolding destiny that awaited her in this magical realm.

THE JOURNEY TO THE HEART

Mia's exploration of Lumina continued, driven by the whispers of the willows and the sense of destiny that pulsed through the forest. The path grew wilder, the air charged with a magical intensity. Lumina seemed to recognize Mia as its chosen one, guiding her toward its heart with unwavering resolve.

As she ventured deeper, the forest's beauty grew more surreal. The trees towered like ancient sentinels, their leaves shimmering with iridescent hues. Luminescent flowers bloomed in abundance, casting an otherworldly glow on the path. Mia marveled at the enchanted flora and fauna, feeling an intimate connection with the magical realm.

Along the way, Mia encountered a variety of mystical creatures. There were delicate fairies with wings that glowed like fireflies, their laughter echoing like tinkling bells. Mischievous sprites flitted about, their translucent forms blending seamlessly with the forest's magic. Mia felt a profound sense of belonging, as if Lumina had always been a part of her.

As she journeyed on, Mia stumbled upon a hidden glade. In the center stood a magnificent tree, its trunk etched with ancient runes. The air around it vibrated with an intense energy, and Mia sensed that this tree held the key to Lumina's heart. With reverence, she approached the tree, feeling its power resonate within her.

Placing her hand on the trunk, Mia closed her eyes and allowed herself to be enveloped by the tree's magic. Visions flashed before her eyes—images of Lumina's past, present, and future. She saw the forest in its prime, brimming with life and magic. She saw the shadows that had crept in, dimming its brilliance. And she saw herself, a beacon of hope, destined to restore Lumina's glory.

When Mia opened her eyes, she felt a renewed sense of purpose. The tree had shared its wisdom, revealing the steps she needed to take to save Lumina. With newfound determination, Mia continued her journey, knowing that the heart of the forest held the answers she sought.

SHADOWS OF THE PAST

Mia's journey through Lumina continued to unravel the complexities of the magical realm. As she ventured deeper, a mysterious presence lingered in the air—a subtle reminder of Lumina's shadowed history. Guided by the whispers of the willows, Mia found herself in an area where the play of light and shadow became more pronounced.

The forest, once radiant and vibrant, now bore the echoes of a past marred by challenges and uncertainties. Mia encountered patches of darkness that seemed to resist the glow of Lumina's natural light. These shadows whispered of forgotten struggles, of a time when Lumina faced threats that dimmed its magical brilliance.

As Mia explored, she stumbled upon ancient ruins, their crumbling structures standing as silent witnesses to the passage of time. Intricate carvings told tales of battles fought and magic lost. Mia sensed a tension in the air, as if Lumina itself yearned to share its secrets, no matter how painful they might be.

Among the ruins, Mia discovered a mural that depicted the kingdom in its prime—a vibrant city bathed in the glow of Lumina's magic. Yet, adjacent to this image, shadowy figures lurked, representing the challenges that had cast a veil over the once-thriving realm.

The shadows seemed to come alive, swirling and coalescing into fleeting forms. Mia felt the weight of Lumina's history—the conflicts, the losses, and the fading of its once-potent magic. As she touched the ancient stones, visions flashed before her eyes—images of struggles against forces that sought to extinguish Lumina's light.

Mia recognized that the journey toward restoration required an understanding of the realm's history. The shadows, though haunting, held the key to unlocking Lumina's true potential. As Mia delved deeper into the enigma, she resolved to face the challenges that lay ahead, driven by the hope of dispelling the shadows and restoring Lumina to its former glory.

THE MOONLIT MEADOW

Mia's exploration of Lumina took an unexpected turn as she followed a winding path that led her to a vast moonlit meadow. Bathed in the gentle glow of moonbeams, the meadow seemed to exist in a time suspended between reality and enchantment. Mia marveled at the celestial dance above, where the moon cast its silver light upon a landscape aglow with luminescent flora.

In the heart of the meadow, Mia encountered a mysterious figure. Cloaked in moonlight, the figure beckoned her forward with an ethereal grace. As they spoke, Mia learned that this enigmatic being was a guardian of Lumina, a custodian of its secrets and a guide for those destined to traverse its mystical realms.

The guardian spoke in riddles and metaphors, revealing fragments of Lumina's destiny. Mia learned that the meadow was a nexus—a place where the threads of fate intertwined, and where Lumina's past, present, and future converged. The guardian alluded to a celestial event, a convergence of cosmic energies that held the potential to shape Lumina's destiny.

As Mia gazed upon the celestial ballet above, the guardian encouraged her to understand the interconnectedness of Lumina's elements—the earth beneath her feet, the celestial bodies above, and the luminous flora that adorned the meadow. The moonlit meadow became a metaphor for Lumina's delicate balance, where each element played a role in the realm's harmony.

Mia grasped the significance of the celestial convergence—a celestial alignment that held the power to amplify Lumina's magic. The guardian urged her to embrace the cosmic energies and harness their potential to usher in a new era for Lumina. The moonlit meadow, with its tranquil beauty and celestial mysteries, became a pivotal space where Mia's understanding deepened, setting the stage for the next phase of her journey.

THE FOREST KEEPER

Mia's journey through Lumina brought her to the heart of the forest, where the ancient magic pulsed with an intensity that resonated within her very soul. The path ahead led to a clearing, bathed in a golden light that seemed to emanate from the core of the realm itself. Here, in the heart of Lumina, Mia encountered the Forest's Keeper—a guardian of unparalleled wisdom and power.

The Forest's Keeper, an ethereal being with eyes that held the knowledge of centuries, welcomed Mia with a knowing smile. The keeper's presence exuded a sense of calm and authority, as if they were the embodiment of Lumina's essence. Mia felt an unspoken connection with the keeper, recognizing them as a guide on her journey.

In a voice that echoed with the resonance of ancient magic, the keeper shared Lumina's story—a tale of a realm that had once thrived in harmony, where magic flowed freely and nature's beauty flourished. But as time passed, challenges arose, and shadows crept in, dimming Lumina's brilliance.

The keeper spoke of the delicate balance that Lumina required—a balance between light and shadow, magic, and reality. Mia learned that her role was to restore this equilibrium, to rekindle the magic that had waned, and to dispel the shadows that threatened the realm's harmony.

With each word, Mia felt a profound sense of purpose. The keeper revealed that Lumina's restoration required a journey through the elemental realms—earth, water, air, and fire. Each element held a fragment of Lumina's essence, and Mia's task was to reunite these fragments, restoring the realm's magic to its former glory.

The Forest's Keeper imparted a final piece of wisdom—an ancient incantation that would guide Mia on her quest. With the keeper's blessing, Mia felt a surge of energy, a connection to the very heart of Lumina. She knew that her journey was far from over, but with the

Forest's Keeper as her guide, she was ready to face the challenges that lay ahead.

As Mia continued her journey through Lumina, the forest seemed to respond to her presence, its magic growing stronger with each step. The path to restoration was fraught with trials, but Mia's determination burned brighter than ever. With the Forest's Keeper's wisdom and the promise of Lumina's rebirth, she ventured forth, ready to embrace the destiny that awaited her in the enchanting realm.

THE ELEMENTAL REALMS

Mia's journey through Lumina entered a new phase as she sought out the four elemental realms—earth, water, air, and fire. Each element held a fragment of Lumina's essence, vital for restoring the realm's magic.

Earth Realm: The Emerald Cavern

Mia's first destination was the Earth Realm, known as the Emerald Cavern. The entrance to the cavern was hidden beneath a canopy of ancient trees, their roots entwining to form a natural archway. As she stepped inside, the air grew cooler, and the walls sparkled with emerald gems that pulsed with a gentle glow.

Deep within the cavern, Mia encountered Earth Elementals—sturdy beings made of rock and soil. They guarded a large, crystalline heart pulsating with green light. To gain the fragment, Mia needed to prove her worth. Through a series of trials, she demonstrated her respect for nature, her strength, and her perseverance. The

Elementals, satisfied with her efforts, bestowed the earth fragment upon her. As she held the fragment, she felt a surge of energy, a promise of the magic it would restore.

Water Realm: The Crystal Lagoon

Next, Mia journeyed to the Water Realm, the Crystal Lagoon. The lagoon was a serene, crystalline body of water surrounded by lush vegetation. Luminescent aquatic creatures swam gracefully, their movements casting shimmering reflections on the water's surface.

Mia dove into the lagoon, guided by water nymphs to the heart of the realm. She reached an underwater grotto where a massive, glowing sapphire awaited. The Water Elementals, ethereal beings flowing like liquid, presented her with challenges that tested her adaptability, calmness under pressure, and purity of spirit. Overcoming these, she earned the water fragment. The sapphire fragment filled her with a deep sense of tranquility and clarity.

Air Realm: The Sky Sanctuary

The Air Realm, or the Sky Sanctuary, was located atop a high mountain. Reaching it required a perilous climb, but the sight that greeted Mia was worth every effort. Floating islands drifted in the air, connected by delicate bridges made of mist and light.

At the sanctuary's center, Mia met the Air Elementals—translucent beings that moved like the wind. They guarded a sphere of pure, swirling air. To obtain the air fragment, Mia had to demonstrate her freedom of spirit, her agility, and her intellect. She faced trials that required her to navigate through intricate mazes of wind currents and solve ancient puzzles. With determination and ingenuity, Mia succeeded and was granted the air fragment. Holding it, she felt a rush of freedom and boundless possibility.

Fire Realm: The Inferno Peak

Mia's final destination was the Fire Realm, known as the Inferno Peak. The path led her through a land of molten lava and scorching heat, where the very air shimmered with intense warmth. At the peak's summit, a grand temple of obsidian and flame awaited.

The Fire Elementals—fiery beings radiating heat and light—guarded a blazing core of fire. To prove herself, Mia faced trials that tested her courage, resilience, and passion. She walked through fire, battled with her inner fears, and demonstrated her unwavering resolve. Her spirit unyielding, Mia earned the fire fragment. As she held the fragment, a fierce energy surged through her, filling her with vitality and determination.

THE CONVERGENCE

With all four elemental fragments in her possession, Mia returned to the heart of Lumina. The Forest's Keeper awaited her in the golden clearing, where the energies of the forest converged. Each fragment pulsed in harmony, resonating with the very essence of Lumina.

Under the Forest's Keeper's guidance, Mia began the ritual to unite the fragments. She placed them in the center of the clearing, where they began to orbit one another, gradually merging their energies. A brilliant light enveloped the forest, and Lumina's magic surged, restoring its vibrancy and brilliance.

As the ritual concluded, the Keeper bestowed upon Mia the title of Lumina's Guardian. She had restored the balance and rekindled the magic that had once faded. Lumina flourished, its beauty and enchantment renewed.

THE SHADOW'S RETURN

Just as peace seemed assured, a dark shadow crept into the forest, the remnants of the old threat that once dimmed Lumina's light. This time, the shadow was stronger, fed by centuries of festering darkness.

Mia, now Lumina's Guardian, faced this new challenge head-on. The shadow manifested into a formidable entity, seeking to reclaim control over the forest. The battle that ensued was fierce, a clash between the light of Lumina and the shadow that sought to consume it.

THE GUARDIAN'S TRIUMPH

Mia drew upon the power of the elements, each fragment within her resonating with Lumina's magic. She wielded the combined energies of earth, water, air, and fire, confronting the shadow with unwavering resolve. The forest, its magic now vibrant, lent its strength to her.

The battle raged on, but Mia's determination never wavered. With a final surge of power, she channeled the essence of Lumina, dispelling the shadow once and for all. The forest rejoiced, its light shining brighter than ever before.

A NEW DAWN

With the shadow vanquished, peace returned to Lumina. The forest thrived under Mia's guardianship, its magic flowing freely once more. Creatures and spirits of Lumina celebrated their restored realm, and the forest flourished in harmony.

Mia stood at the heart of the forest, the weight of her journey settling into a sense of accomplishment and fulfillment. She knew that her role as Lumina's Guardian was only beginning, but she was ready. The whispers of the willows, the wisdom of the Forest's Keeper, and the essence of the elements would guide her.

As dawn broke over Lumina, casting a golden light across the enchanted realm, Mia embraced the new beginning. The forest was alive with magic and possibility, and Mia, its steadfast guardian, stood ready to protect and nurture the realm she had come to love.

LOST IN LUMINA

www.ingramcontent.com/pod-product-compliance
Lightning Source LLC
LaVergne TN
LVHW051923060526
838201LV00060B/4146